I0747412

BY MARIA CAIAZZA

MODERN TALES OF OLD SERIES

Heartless
The Seven Ravens

OTHER BOOKS BY MARIA CAIAZZA

Be Still My Undying Heart

BE STILL MY
UNDYING HEART

BE STILL MY UNDYING HEART

A DARK FANTASY ROMANCE NOVELETTE

MARIA CAIAZZA

ESCAPISM
ENTERTAINMENT
LLC

For Sara, who had to listen to me babble about this for months.

~~SHOPPING LIST~~

TRIGGER WARNINGS

(This list includes spoilers.)

This book contains subject matter that might be difficult for some readers, including suicidal ideation, grief/loss of a loved one (wife), gaslighting/emotional abuse by a spouse, physical abuse/domestic violence (off page), police corruption, LOTS of pining, drinking/alcoholism, premeditated murder, unrequited love, lust for a married person, MMC does not get the girl, no happy ending.

Your mental health matters.

HAUNTED BY MEMORIES

DALTON'S GREATEST BLESSING WAS ALSO his greatest curse. At one time, his eternal life granted to him by a sorcerer sounded like everything he could ever dream of. He imagined that world in his mind's eye now, the same way it appeared centuries ago. The only reason he didn't take his own life and escape his bodily imprisonment was cowardice.

And dare he say hope.

It was a fool's hope, but it was his to hold on to. If he lived long enough, he might hold his dream in his hands.

When he closed his eyes, he let the scene play out before him. This luxury wasn't one he allowed himself often. He chose one day a year to indulge. In equal parts, he considered it an act of grief and motivation. Without this, he couldn't fathom how much longer he could tolerate this sack of flesh he walked around in.

His first and favorite memory was her smile; it lit up every room, just like she did with his heart. Along with the idea of her smile, came her laugh. Perhaps it was the length of her absence, but it reminded him of a songbird's singing: high, staccato, and joyful. He longed to hear that sound again one day. Even after centuries, he could feel her body pressed against his in an embrace. The fresh, herbal scent of her hair haunted him differently than the kitchen's emptiness the first week she went away.

Yes, he preferred to picture her alive and well. She merely left on a trip one day. Somewhere along the way, she'd gotten lost and hadn't found her way home yet. Normally, he dared not think about the sickness that ravaged her body. He watched the color drain from her cheeks and the light die in her eyes, and he begged whatever gods may listen to take him instead. In every lifetime, he would trade his life for hers without hesitation.

With her last breaths, he watched his dreams fade away. He held onto her as he grieved *what was* and *what could've been*. The tombstone he erected still stood, but he seldom visited. To visit her resting place rooted him to the past while he tried desperately to latch onto thoughts of his future. No, *their* future.

On a long enough timeline, he knew she would return to him. No concrete evidence for reincarnation existed; he checked. But when they met, they experienced an immediate connection and familiarity that was altogether too natural. After that, he was certain they'd known each other in a past life. Now, he clung to life as long as tolerable, waiting for the day he found her beautiful soul again.

His eyes opened, and they settled upon the calendar hanging on the wall, marking the date. It was one forever ingrained in his mind. He celebrated her birthday every year. A soul like hers deserved a day to shine, and in his head, she did.

His attention turned to a reproduction of her portrait that he hung above the fireplace. Her eyes pierced his very being. He deserved her judgement and her scorn. Even though they planned on experiencing this transformation together, he was a killer, and she was not. Her soul remained unblemished while his grew darker each passing day. Such was his life as a creature who must consume human blood to survive.

"Happy birthday, Vanessa. I hope you'll return home soon, my love. This vacation of yours has become dreadfully long, and this old fool misses you."

PHANTOM OF HOPE

DAYS BLURRED TOGETHER, AS THEY DO with age. Ever since his transformation during the eighteenth century, Dalton took to moving every decade. Otherwise, people grew suspicious when they noticed his agelessness.

On a dreary, overcast day with on and off rain, he chanced a walk down the historic downtown area of his latest home. It was a lovely little place with brick buildings broken up by ones with colorful siding and inviting windows full of interesting wares. There were a few run-down buildings, but overall, the town obviously made painstaking efforts to revitalize the area, keeping the town full of charm.

He stumbled as he passed an empty storefront with a black and white printed sign taped to the glass door, but he didn't trip up because of something wrong with his gait or a flaw in the sidewalk. No, this was much different.

His hand moved up to touch the center of his chest where his heart stood still, waiting. Logically, he knew he stood waiting for something that would never come. Didn't he feel it just now? A heartbeat, he knew it was real.

"Sir, are you okay?" a young man in, perhaps, his early thirties, asked from beside him.

Dalton's attention shifted, and he looked up at the other man in surprise. His interactions with humans nowadays were transactional. He accepted a delivery from a driver or spoke with a cashier, but he couldn't remember the last time he conversed with anybody outside of the scope of their job duties. He lived a solitary existence. Most of the time, he spoke to himself out of sheer boredom.

"I," he started. "Yes, I think so. My heart beat-"

He couldn't tell the man his heart beat for the first time in three hundred years. Otherwise, he may end up in the emergency room or a psychiatric ward.

"Strangely," he finished. "It's gone now, whatever it was."

The man's grim expression transformed into an inviting grin. He clapped Dalton on the shoulder. "Good to hear. Glad you're okay, man."

"Ah, yes. Thank you," he said, still jarred by the interaction.

Before he escaped, the other man asked, "Say, this is a pretty small town, and I don't remember seeing you around here before. Are you here visiting?"

Dalton raised a hand in a gentle stopping motion. "No. I've moved here recently, so I thought I'd wander around to get a lay of the land."

Of all things the young man could do, the vampire couldn't believe he took his hand into a firm shake. This whole interaction astounded him.

"Well, it's good to have ya. Welcome," the young man said. "I'm Cody. My wife and I just leased this place."

He followed the gesture Cody made with his thumb towards the empty shop. For the first time, he noticed the lights on inside the establishment. A counter stood on the left side of the shop, inviting customers towards it with a window panel to view edible wares and an espresso maker behind it, but no tables or chairs filled the otherwise empty dining area. His eyes gravitated to the simple sign taped on the door. *Coming Soon: Bakery.*

"I hope you'll stop by for the grand opening. She's worked hard to make it a success, and she's nervous nobody will show, even though the mayor promised to stop by."

"The mayor?" Dalton asked. "This town is smaller than I thought."

Cody laughed. "It's a tight-knit community. See you around- I'm sorry, what was your name again?"

"I didn't say."

"Alright. Next time then," he said, letting himself into the yet-to-be-opened bakery.

Dalton stared after Cody, watching him head into the kitchen where commercial appliances gleamed. He lingered in the window, staring without seeing. It came and went so fast it didn't feel real. Did his heart really beat, or did he imagine it?

He stared at the window long enough until he noticed reflections from other passersby. Reminded of his need for secrecy, he kept moving. His hand moved up to his chest where he rubbed it, lingering on his concern.

Perhaps, he should revisit his research on vampirism. By his best approximation, he studied the subject a century ago. Perhaps after all this time, somebody discovered something new about their kind. Whether it ended as a waste of time or not, he decided following through was worth the effort. At worst, what did it hurt? All he did was waste his infinite time. Besides, if he couldn't figure it out through study, the phenomenon already passed. With no real reason to worry, forgetting it ever happened sounded like a viable option as well.

SPECTRE FROM THE PAST

FOR VAMPIRES, TIME IS A LIMINAL SPACE; they exist within its confines, but it's something passed through rather than lingered in. Dalton's contacts in the supernatural world loved hearing from him, but most of his kind were possessive of their worldly belongings. Unfortunately, his thirst for untold knowledge sent him on a fool's errand the world over that took him away from home for a month.

His frustration festered as he returned, but he stayed positive. The heart beating sensation he experienced never recurred, so he wrote it off as nothing more than an outlier in an otherwise uneventful afterlife.

At least, he spent time in familiar company. His gratitude for his friends' companionship lessened the blow from his unsuccessful pursuit. Cody seemed kind enough, but only other immortals could understand Dalton. Humanity passed him by long ago, and a stranger couldn't change that.

It took him three and a half hours to make it back to his home after he flew into the closest airport. He chose the location because of price and location. Years ago, he decided to avoid major feeding hubs. With his abilities, he flew there quickly while avoiding suspicion thanks to modern day technology. Of course, the rise of facial recognition technology concerned him, but with magic on his side, he would worry about police investigations and criminal charges if they became relevant.

As he pulled into town, the signage over the bridge made his lips tip up. Dalton hadn't lived here long, but he grew rather fond of the place in short order. It felt like no time passed since he last arrived. Small towns rarely changed; this universal truth, he learned decades ago.

He turned off the main road into his neighborhood, spotting a few subtle changes to home decor as fall transitioned to winter. Some houses still wore Halloween decorations while others already donned their whites and blues, reds and greens. A younger vampire might feel a festive thrill, but all it meant was another year passing without finding Vanessa.

His very soul longed for his wife.

Thump-thump.

In a split second, he checked for other cars behind him and slammed on his brakes. Why and how did this keep happening? He pulled over and scanned the neighborhood. Nothing stuck out as significant. Why did the cursed organ choose to palpitate here? What made the anomaly happen again?

During his vampiric afterlife, he never experienced this wretched heart beating before. He spoke to his contacts and nobody had evidence an undead heart could restart. It made no sense. No external stimuli triggered this change. The only common factor was this town.

Deflated, Dalton climbed back into his SUV while considering his options. Research garnered no help, and he didn't care to extend his reach within the highly political vampire community. The last thing he needed was some nosy immortal pricks getting into his business.

He could always move. This curiosity didn't begin until after he arrived here. If he left, he'd likely never experience the odd fluttering ever again. However, the idea of repacking his recently unpacked belongings grated on his nerves. He hated the mere idea of the task.

His final remaining option irritated him almost as much as the previous two. Was sloth a sin if he chose it over other options with all things weighed in equal parts? Did it matter if vampirism already damned his soul?

Irritated at his tumultuous thoughts, Dalton fired his car up and finished the drive home. As always, eternity spanned in front of him. Decisions could wait.

DOPPELGÄNGER OF DESIRE

AFTER ABOUT A WEEK OF ENJOYING THE comfort and privacy of his new-to-him house, Dalton became restless, ready to venture outside again. The rainy season began while he travelled, so he could leave whenever he wanted. When he considered his options, nothing interested him.

Eventually, he convinced himself to leave despite his apathy. He learned that shutting himself in drove him to madness long ago. Determined to escape the confines of his homey prison, he threw on a waterproof coat and headed out the door. Walking often helped clear his head. Remembering the historic district's charm, he decided to explore the storefronts more thoroughly. The thrift store looked like it carried vintage records, which he'd love to add to his collection.

As he set off, he chuckled to himself. How could he forget that most people avoided going outside when it rained? He considered driving but decided against it. It would only take a few extra minutes, and he knew surrounding himself with nature would lift his spirits.

He noticed heavy traffic on his walk. It surprised him. From his experience thus far, this place was quiet and unexciting. What could've caused such a large crowd to congregate?

Part of him wanted to return later, but curiosity won out. After walking here, he needed to know what the hubbub was about. He watched several people in groups of ones and twos cross the street and bustle over to an unfamiliar storefront. His eyebrows drew together as he eyed the building. Why didn't he remember the shop? An ornate wrought iron sign rocked with the gentle breeze, drawing his attention. *Tess's Treats,* the words read, surrounded by the outline of a cupcake.

Now, he understood his lack of recognition. Cody and his wife planned to open a bakery. When he visited last, Tess's Treats didn't exist. It turned into a successful business while he travelled. Even though he only needed blood to sustain him, this sounded like the perfect opportunity to support a local business.

Dalton crossed the street and stepped in line. It trailed out the door, but it moved fast enough. Several customers filtered out as Cody taped a sign in the window that read, *Now Hiring,* before hustling over to bus empty tables.

The man looked harried compared to his composure from a month earlier. He didn't know when the bakery's grand opening happened, but it must've been busy for a few days for them to hire help already. With several people ahead of him in line, he grabbed his phone for some research. The first page that appeared was a Facebook page. Tess's Treats opened three days prior, and it filled a void of baked goods for several surrounding towns.

"*No wonder they're busy*," he thought.

Dalton felt a pair of fingers tap his shoulder.

"Hey, buddy. Pay attention."

He looked up from his phone and noticed the line moved up about four people while he distracted himself.

"Apologies."

As he wandered forward into the warmth of the bakery, he felt that cursed heartbeat again. It made him want to leave out of spite, forgoing the pleasure of smelling buttery sweetness in the air surrounding him. After buying his treat, he swore he'd leave this thrice damned town so he never felt the wretched thrumming sensation ever again.

"Sorry about that!" a woman said in an airy soprano as she slid fresh scones into the viewing case. She removed a pair of gloves and tossed them in a trash can, rubbing her hands on her apron before operating the register.

Upon hearing the voice, Dalton's head whipped up. He hadn't heard *her* voice in centuries, but he recognized it immediately. Everything about her lingered in his mind forever. No matter what form she took, he would know her. That voice… this woman… was *his* Vanessa. He remembered her perfection vividly, and her new form was the same.

His world instantly bent and reshaped itself around her. Nothing else mattered.

He couldn't breathe; as usual, she'd taken that ability away. She'd braided and pinned up her honeyed brown hair into a bun, but pieces fell out and framed her heart-shaped face and hazel eyes. Dalton didn't need to look. Of all his memories, his recollection of her was absolutely flawless. Still, he couldn't look away.

She pulled at him like a magnet, and with each customer moving out of the way, it somehow grew stronger. How could he survive reuniting with her? If he lost her now, she'd ruin him. In her absence, life didn't exist. Only survival remained. He lived half a life without her, seeing her again reminded him of the truth. She didn't know it, but she cursed him with her presence. He forgot what living felt like, and he didn't remember until she returned to him. One last customer stood in front of his quarry, and he wanted to push them away and feast his eyes on her like a starving man devouring a meal. His near infinite patience whittled down to nothing in the agonizing seconds before she was his.

Thump-thump.

There it was again, the confounding feeling. He understood now. His body tried to tell him before, but he didn't listen. He didn't *know*. How could he? No other vampire lost their loved one before they both turned. At least, no other *living* vampire experienced it. They all lost themselves to grief so *he* could discover the magic of finding his once-lost love.

He stood in front of her. When did the last customer leave? Why couldn't he remember anything besides the feeling of her beside him with their hands entwined?

"Thanks for your patience," she said, finally looking up at him with a pleasant smile.

They locked eyes, sharing a connection that made the din around them go quiet. To Dalton, who'd lived through entire lifetimes, this moment lasted longer than the centuries that passed between her last breath and this greeting. Time stilled, and he knew he'd remember their second meeting after millennia. He swore he'd never lose her once he found her again, and he intended to keep his promise.

A loud buzzing from the kitchen startled them both. The haze they both fell victim to faded away, and the sounds of the bustling bakery and exuberant guests returned.

"Oh, that's the chocolate croissants. I'll be right back."

Dalton stood there in shock as she ran off. She must've felt it too. They shared this bond, right?

"Oh, sorry to keep you waiting," a familiar, masculine voice said. "What can I get for you?"

It felt like a slap in the face when he realized. This was Cody, the baker's husband. Of course, he finally found Vanessa's reincarnation, but she returned in a form wholly untouchable. She could never be his.

SHADOW OF A DREAM

CODY STARED DALTON DOWN FOR several beats before grinning. "Hey, man. It's been a while. How're you feeling? Better, I hope."

"Y- yes," Dalton barely stammered out.

"Good. Did you ever see a doctor about your heart?"

Blindsided by his situation, he couldn't cobble together a response. Every single piece of medical terminology he learned over the years escaped him, and an empty sieve remained.

"Ah, yes. I'm right as rain," he said, clearing his throat. "Can I get a black coffee and a lemon blueberry scone?"

"Yeah, you need a caffeine pick-me-up. You didn't drive here, did you?"

"Walked," he said, keeping it simple while his thoughts did gymnastics.

Cody turned around and poured coffee into a paper cup. He set it down and dropped the confection in a to-go bag. "Hey man, it's crazy busy, and I don't want to cause a scene. Next time you visit, I'll buy."

Dalton handed the other man a twenty and grabbed his order. "Keep the change."

He didn't give Cody a chance to respond before retreating. Right now, he wanted to fly far away as fast as his wings could carry him, but excited guests crowded the street, forcing him to walk.

The further away he got, the faster Dalton strode. Before long, he ran as fast as he dared for fear of revealing his supernatural abilities. He arrived home, and it took a monumental effort to unlock the door instead of forcing his way in. Once inside, he fell into his couch where he sat heavily from a weight entirely different from weariness.

After several lifetimes, he watched his life's goal crumble before him. He hated that he would survive this. He wanted to die of a broken heart and reincarnate with her where they could live and be happy together again. Curse this feeling. Curse his undying body. And damn his beating heart to hell.

How did this happen? Nobody controlled when or where he moved. It was instinct. Some sense buried deep inside him brought him here, but why would he come here when another man stole his heart's desire?

Part of him wondered if he should leave.

His attention returned to the food in his hands. It reminded him of their home, filled with the delightful fragrance of her cooking. At least, he could visit her often. He could ensure her safety. If he couldn't claim her, he could give her a good life until she succumbed to old age.

It wasn't ideal, but he could draw satisfaction from watching her enjoy a long, fulfilling life. All he wanted was her happiness, even if it wasn't with him.

Demons Lurking

DALTON WALKED INTO THE BAKERY JUST after opening at six. He preferred it quiet, and coming in early ensured he never waded through a throng of hungry customers again. The yeasty sweetness of fresh baked goods washed over him as he entered. It filled him with the feeling of hearth and home, a once-distant memory from his life with Vanessa.

"Good morning, Tess," he said as he wiped his feet off on the mat.

She smiled at him and turned around to pour him a cup of coffee without asking. "Good morning. What're you eating today?"

He glanced at the pastry case and hummed. "Am I really this predictable already? I should order something else to drink for once. I'll have one of the chocolate chip muffins today."

Tess pulled out a white porcelain plate and placed the muffin on it with a pair of tongs. "You don't need to change your routine. It's okay to enjoy coffee. I don't know how you've avoided gaining weight, though."

"A healthy metabolism," he lied. Truth be told, no amount of consumption would change his physical form, but he couldn't tell a human that.

"That'll catch up to you. Be careful, okay? I can't afford my best customer dying of a heart attack."

He laughed. "I'm hardly your best customer. I thought you were speaking with a corporate client?"

She shook her head. "Didn't go through."

"That's a shame. What happened, if you don't mind my asking?"

She sighed, frustration palpable. "I got my hopes up. It's just Cody blowing smoke again."

He nodded and used the moment's silence between them to hand her another twenty-dollar bill. Coming here daily and never requesting change was becoming an expensive habit. Even though it pained him to hear about her husband causing her grief, his dislike of the man felt justified. After their second meeting, Dalton encountered the man at the register four more times before the cretin went back to his day job. Not once did the insufferable prick actually follow through on treating him to a complimentary visit.

"If it helps, I work remote, so you're technically feeding an office every day," he said. It wasn't true, but it made her laugh.

"Thank you," she said. "It makes me feel a little better."

The bell at the front door jingled. He grabbed his meal and wandered over to his favorite seat in the back corner of the shop. He liked monitoring things until Tessa's assistant arrived. She could spend an hour alone, but it gave him peace of mind knowing he could protect her if somebody robbed the place. Her employee came in a few minutes before their morning rush started, and nobody in their right mind would pull something with multiple witnesses.

It may be simple, but he ensured her safety each morning. He just hoped she didn't burn herself out. The bakery operated daily, and he worried she neglected working rest into her schedule. If he noticed she needed a break, he planned to suggest a reduction of hours or vacation. Hiring extra hands too quickly risked the bakery, so he hoped she listened to his advice if the time came.

He peeled the wrapper from the muffin and took a bite. The buttery sweetness burst across his tongue. It had a fluffy yet cakey texture to it, and for the thousandth time, he wondered if she attended culinary school. He washed down his bite with a sip of piping hot coffee and relaxed as he enjoyed the hum of quiet conversation between Tessa and her customers along with the quaint ambiance surrounding him.

There were ten square cafe tables arranged throughout the shop with four placed next to a long, upholstered bench seat along the wall opposite the cash register. He preferred the comfort of the bench over the decorative chairs sitting opposite. The chairs pinched in the wrong places after sitting for too long. On the wall, watercolors of bright-colored flowers hung, bringing color and vibrance to the otherwise forgettable storefront. At least, the only criticism he had was cheap, uncomfortable chairs.

He enjoyed his breakfast in silence, watching cars drive by outside while customers wandered in for their morning fix. During a lull in activity, Dalton stole glances at Tessa's slender form. He remembered feeling her curves against his as he held her close. Gods, he missed her.

"Did you say something?" she asked from behind the counter.

He shook his head and pulled out his phone to give him something else to look at. "Not unless you're a mind reader."

She laughed and waved him off. The chime of a timer dinged in the kitchen, and she disappeared into the back.

Before long, the bell at the front rang, and Dalton saw Tess's assistant, Brittany, removing her coat as she headed into the back. "Sorry I'm late," she said.

"Don't worry about it. It's been a slow morning so far," Tess replied.

"They're never that slow!" she called from the kitchen, coming out a moment later as she tied the strings of her apron around her waist. "My oldest had a breakdown in the car line at school. Remind me to buy his teacher a bottle of booze before winter break, will you?"

They both laughed while Dalton cleaned his table, folding a napkin and placing it on the plate. He picked up his dish and carried it to the front. As he placed the plate in the used items bin, he met Tess's gaze. Keeping his secret pained him, but he didn't want to ruin her happy marriage. It felt rude to just leave after locking eyes.

"I've been meaning to ask. Did you go to culinary school, or is baking a skill you learned on your own?" he asked.

"I apprenticed at a bakery in France for a while, but I didn't finish," she said with a shrug. "Life had other plans."

"Well, I'm glad you followed your heart," he said, giving her a nod and stepping away. He almost made it out the door before realizing he left his coffee at the table, so he turned around to grab it.

"Girl, is that *another* bruise? You need to stop hauling around the bags of flour and sugar and have that man of yours do it instead," Brittany said.

"I'm a bit of a klutz," Tess said, rubbing her forearm where Brittany spotted a purple bruise about the size of a quarter.

"When they're back in season, I'm going to the Dollar Store and buying a bunch of pool noodles to accident proof the kitchen."

Tess ignored her and turned her attention to Dalton, "Nice to see you again, have a good day!"

He held the door in one hand and his cup in the other, so he tipped his cup at her. "See you next time," he said, knowing he'd return tomorrow.

FIEND IN DISGUISE

THE HOLIDAYS GREW CLOSER, AND THE streets were thick with shoppers hunting for gifts for their loved ones. Even though Dalton didn't celebrate this commercialized holiday, he longed for somebody to enjoy the passing of each year with. He didn't know how long he could endure this limbo after Tess departed this world again.

He arrived a minute or two before opening, but he tested the door, regardless. It startled him when it moved. He hesitated but decided that a human would step inside. In order to stay under the radar, he acted like a human. He sat in the lobby and stared at the black and white diner tile while he waited for the shop to open.

"I'm not saying that, Cody," Tess said from the kitchen. "I'm literally killing myself doing all of this on my own. You never listen. I need support."

"I can't believe you would even say that," he responded without hesitation. "After all I've done for you, you think I don't help? What about that first week? I was there every day. My job paid for all of this. How is that not supportive?"

"That's not what I meant!"

"What did you mean, then? Is working a job that pays the bills not enough? What would be enough for you, Tessa? Why is my best not enough?"

She sounded like she was ready to scream or cry. Her voice cracked as she said, "Doing your job is great, but you don't help with anything else. Why is it always money with you? I thought we were partners."

"We're not partners? I do so much. You just take me for granted." He fell silent for a second.

"You made me late again. I've got to go so I can pay for your little pet project."

"I'm not-"

A door slammed, followed by a frustrated growl.

Dalton heard sniffles; then, water running in the kitchen. He wondered why Cody called the bakery a pet project. Even though he didn't intimately know the financials, business looked good. Did he not understand that investments took time? It would shock him if Tess's Treats stayed in the red past the three-year mark. Unfortunately, not everybody knew business like him, but he wouldn't allow the bakery to fail on his watch.

About five minutes later, Tess stepped out of the kitchen and stopped in her tracks when she noticed Dalton waiting in the lobby.

"You didn't hear any of that, did you?" she asked.

He stood up and walked over to her. "I know I am a customer, but if you need anything, I would move heaven and earth for your safety and happiness."

She marched past him and poured coffee into a to-go cup. With tongs, she placed two pastries into a paper bag and handed the lot to him. "I think you should go."

His fingers brushed hers as he grabbed the items. The otherwise still heart in his chest throbbed twice in quick succession. He hoped she felt it too. His heart beat for her, and it always would. Without another word, he left the bakery behind.

WISHES AND DJINNS

EVEN THOUGH HE WASN'T WELCOME, Dalton couldn't shy away from Tess's siren call. It hurt for her to distance herself after his faux pas. Part of him wished he could go back and lie instead. This whole wretched ordeal felt like a cautionary tale about being careful what you wish for. Sometimes, he dreamt of letting himself succumb to loneliness. He wanted to reincarnate *with* her rather than wait, but the time for decisions passed long ago.

He let himself into the lonely bakery, but unlike other mornings, the shop looked abandoned. The pastries weren't waiting and the chairs still hung upside down on their tables. Panicking, he glanced at his watch. It was five minutes after opening, so she wouldn't argue about his presence, right?

"Be right out!" Tess called.

Her unexpected shout made him jump, but his shoulder muscles released tension after hearing her. He didn't think their relationship could handle another setback. She barely spoke to him, and it broke him more each time she averted her gaze instead of meeting his.

Dalton watched the kitchen door, waiting for her entrance. When she poked her head out from the back, he expected her to greet him. Her previous warmth waned considerably after he overheard the argument, but he stood by his decision to express his concern. She could hate him as long as he could keep her safe.

Instead of exiting the kitchen, she ducked back inside with an audible sigh. "Can you help him, please? I just can't right now."

"Uh, sure."

Confused, Brittany shuffled out of the kitchen. When she noticed Dalton, she smiled.

"Good morning," she said. "What can I get for you?"

"I'll have a large coffee and a cheese danish, please."

He watched her pour the coffee and took it from her asking, "To what do I owe the pleasure this early in the morning?"

"Tess needs me to open the shop for her while she's at an appointment in a couple days. She's training me on how to open." She shrugged, running into the back to retrieve his pastry.

"Well, it's good to know she has you to look after things while she's away," he said, handing her his customary overpayment. "I worry she's overworking herself. It's good to hear she plans on taking time off."

"I feel the same way. See you next time."

He nodded and retreated to his favorite table where he removed the chair opposite the bench and placed it on the floor. It would look suspicious to change his routine, so he decided to stick around until a normal hour.

After a moment, Brittany returned to the back. In no time, they were chatting again. The acoustics in the kitchen carried sound well; he heard their entire exchange, even when they tried to keep their voices down. He tried to ignore it, but when their conversation wandered away from business to a discussion about him, he couldn't help but keep an ear open.

"What happened with him again?" Brittany asked. "It's been weeks. You never struck me as one to hold a grudge."

"He eavesdropped on an argument between Cody and I."

"How did that happen?"

Metal utensils clattered before she said, "He came in the door while we were in the back."

"So the shop was open."

Tess tutted. "No. Well, yes. I suppose. I don't know."

"That doesn't sound confident."

"I unlocked the door early and forgot. Cody and I fought. He came inside and overheard some sensitive topics."

Brittany hummed in the sarcastic way women do before calling somebody out. "And how cold has it been outside?"

Tess must've dropped something since a loud crash followed the question. "He heard us airing out our dirty laundry. It's embarrassing. He didn't even apologize."

"Neither have you."

"I don't even remember his name."

"That, I can help you with," Brittany laughed.

Tess sounded nervous when she said, "You're terrifying. You know that, right?"

"Oh, I know."

"Are you going to tell me your plan, at least?" Tess asked, her voice pitching higher in curiosity.

Brittany laughed. "And tell you how I'll solve your problems with the thoughtful, cute, good tipper who visits every day? Never."

"Stop it."

"I only speak the truth, girl. Like, oh no, a hot guy cares about my feelings. Shut up and stop pretending you didn't like the attention."

He couldn't tell what happened while they were in the kitchen, but it quickly devolved into giggles.

SPIRIT OF FRIENDSHIP

BRITTANY'S ABILITY TO DIFFUSE situations and problem solve impressed even a centuries-old vampire. The day after Dalton overheard the conversation between the pair, a business card raffle jar appeared on the counter. He fought not to laugh. Her solution was truly ingenious. As the proprietor poured his morning coffee, he dropped a business card inside.

"This was a great idea," he said. "It's a great way to increase business and learn about your client base."

Tess handed him his coffee and opened the pastry case next. "Brittany deserves the credit. She's a godsend."

"We're lucky to have her around." He glanced at the display case, trying to decide. He imagined the smooth texture of her banana bread along with the crunchy bitterness of walnuts, and his mouth watered.

Before he could ask, she swiped a piece out of its tray and plated it.

"How did you guess?"

"You might as well have screamed it," she responded with a laugh. "You're an odd one sometimes, you know?"

He placed a twenty on the counter and took the plate. Part of him wanted to continue, but this was the most they'd spoken since the incident. He didn't want to push his luck. Instead, he retreated to his usual table.

"Um, wait," Tess said nervously.

He stopped in his tracks and turned back around. "Is something wrong?"

"Yes. Well, no. I just-"

She sighed.

"I'm sorry. What happened wasn't your fault. It could've been anybody coming in out of the cold. I shouldn't have blamed you."

A soft smile spread across his face. "I already forgave you. The fault is mine for causing you more distress during a difficult situation."

"Thank you for worrying about me. We're almost strangers, but I know you'd help if I asked."

"We see each other every day. You are important to me, and I would do anything to ensure your happiness," he said as openly as he could. In all honesty, she was the only person he cared about, but he didn't need to voice it.

The bell on the shop door rang as another customer entered. He inclined his head at Tess and sat in his usual seat. If he could kiss whichever deity created Brittany, he would do it right on the lips. That woman deserved a raise.

FALLEN ANGEL

CHRISTMAS PASSED WITH LITTLE fanfare, and on the twenty-sixth, Dalton gratefully returned to his usual routine. Even if they only discussed the weather and surface-level subjects, Tess brought joy into his days. He looked forward to their conversations, regardless of length or content.

Another dreary and wet morning greeted him, but he didn't mind. The weather helped guard his secret, even if he couldn't leave home much during summer.

When he entered the bakery, he wiped his shoes and glanced around. He guessed Tess was working in the back. Taking a seat, he pulled out his phone to wait, trying not to salivate over the delicious scents wafting out of the kitchen. A minute passed before footsteps rounded the corner out of the kitchen.

"Oh, Dalton. Could you please help me? I can't lift this tray for the display case."

He stood without hesitation. In a few strides, he entered the kitchen and waited for directions.

"Are you alright?" he asked, torn between voicing his worry and remaining silent. "You usually handle this fine without me."

"I, uh, hurt my back," she said hesitantly.

Dalton hummed at her response, but he lifted the tray and brought it out front, nonetheless. His past with Tess's original incarnation left him completely unprepared for this iteration. Vanessa used to tell him everything, but back then, they were married. She and Cody shared that bond now, but he suspected she didn't communicate with her husband as much as she did before. He overheard their argument, and occasionally, she brought up the grief Cody put her through. It broke his heart. If he could save her from the pain and replace it with love, he would.

He looked at her with a mixture of sadness and concern. At the risk of ruining their freshly mended relationship, he asked, "Why would you lie about your injury?"

Tess stared at him for several seconds before walking past him and pouring a cup of coffee. She handed him the drink and pulled a chocolate croissant from the case.

"No charge today. Thank you for helping me."

Instead of taking the items, he gripped her wrists with tender firmness. "I can't help you unless you tell me what's happened."

"I can't," she said, with her eyes locked on his. They were wide, and her muscles tensed and subtly shook. He heard her heart hammer in her chest.

"Can't you? Or won't you?" he asked, measuring his tone and remaining calm. If he could become ill, he would. Humans reacted with fear when a vampire grew too close. He thought she was immune, but he fooled himself.

"I can't. There's nothing to say." Her eyes cut away from his.

He released her wrists and plucked the coffee and croissant from her hands. "Very well. Please let me know if I can help before Brittany arrives."

"I will. Thank you, Dalton."

He stepped away and claimed his usual spot. They should print a, *Reserved for Dalton*, sign. When she said his name, he still got a thrill of excitement. Thank goodness for Brittany and her tricks. Otherwise, neither of them would've learned his name.

As he watched Tess work, he noticed her stiff movements. His heart ached for her, and he wished he could help. Her health and wellbeing were of the utmost importance to him, but if she wouldn't communicate with him, he couldn't fix anything. Hell, he didn't even know what he was up against.

He hoped she would rely on him when she was ready.

REMEMBERING

FANTASMS

THE NEW YEAR BROUGHT A LAYER OF snow thick enough that Dalton considered avoiding his daily routine altogether. Over the years, he'd driven through snow plenty, but idiots always ventured out on these days, especially in places where snow was infrequent at best. The idea of Tess venturing out and traversing the unplowed streets at three in the morning to get the bakery open wrenched at his soul's frayed edges. If she risked her life to open the shop, he should at least drop by and overpay her.

He ensured he looked human by bundling up. Of course, he felt the chill, but with no functional circulatory system, he didn't fear frostbite or other negative side effects of exposure. He was already dead; the weather wouldn't kill him.

Usually, he left space for guests to park closest to the entrance, but a normal person would take the nearest stall. A part of Dalton hated over-analyzing his decisions, but it became a game. He asked himself what normal people would do and considered a human's mindset. His biggest hurdle was age and not experiencing human life before cars, cell phones, and other modern conveniences. It forced him to think critically, and sometimes, he created scenarios in his head. Most of the time, he discovered the correct answer independently. Sometimes, he embarrassed himself or needed to explain his strangeness, but it grew far less necessary after years of practice.

Dalton's lips curled when he remembered visiting a modern theater for the first time and causing a ruckus when he realized the cinema no longer hired usherettes. He laughed at himself before sliding out of his seat and carefully striding to the door over slick sidewalk.

As he entered the bakery, the warmth alongside the smell of pastries beckoned him like the pied piper ensnared his quarry. It may look and feel different from his memories, but this was home. Wherever she called home was his as well, and it always would be. Centuries ago, he would arrive after work, and she already prepared dinner. He missed those days more than anything. Sometimes, he yearned for the feeling of her body beside his while they sat in front of the fire and he read her a passage from their favorite book.

"Good morning!" Tess said as she wheeled around the corner. "I'm so glad you made it safely. It's awful outside."

"I worried more about you. Getting here early to bake must've been treacherous."

"It was." The wince she replied with spoke volumes.

Dalton wanted to reprimand her for risking herself today, but he knew she'd brush his worries off, founded or not. "I'm glad you made it here uneventfully."

She turned away and grabbed a cup, filling it with coffee, which had a plume of steam wafting off the top. After setting the lid in place, she spun around and handed it to him.

Their fingers brushed upon taking the cup. A fresh pang of longing struck him. He missed holding her hand, rubbing his thumb across the back, squeezing it to share silent reassurance. Of course, he missed her presence, but the little gestures hurt the most. Sometimes, he even wished to hear her snoring.

He stifled the levity the thought summoned before he said, "Thank you. This should warm me up."

She shivered and rubbed her arms. "I hope it does. It's *too* cold today."

"Turn up the thermostat. If you're stuck here all day, get comfortable."

"I agree," she said with a smile, bustling into the back. She returned when renewed heat rushed through the vents overhead. "What would you like to eat today?"

"Honestly?" he asked. "Something I know you don't have."

"Oh? What is that?"

Dalton laughed at her enthusiastic response. "I would love a croissant breakfast sandwich."

Tess hummed. "I think I can make that happen, actually."

She walked away before pausing. "Why didn't you ask about this sooner? I could've been selling breakfast sandwiches all along!"

He laughed and shook his head. "It's your bakery. Who am I to dictate your menu?"

"Oh, and the potential to bring in the lunch crowd with pre-made club sandwiches. I've been missing out," she muttered to herself as she walked back into the kitchen.

He could hear utensils and pans clattering as she worked. After a few minutes, he wondered what she was doing, but he wouldn't interrupt a master at work. Vanessa would've swatted him away if he even offered his help. He believed this incarnation would do the same. Sometimes, both versions were so alike it hurt.

"Any food allergies or dislikes I should know about?" she called from the back.

"Garlic."

Of course, he couldn't explain, but he should tell her, or she might accidentally kill him with a breakfast sandwich.

She shrieked in dismay. "I am *so* sorry! I'm Italian. Without garlic, I may keel over and die."

"I miss the stuff. It was an adult onset allergy," he said as the scent of bacon ensnared his senses. "That smells phenomenal."

"I hope you don't mind, but I'm making two. I can't smell this without tasting one."

"No offense taken. I think I'd do the same."

Their conversation grew quiet again. He sat and sipped his coffee, savoring the heat after enduring the chill. His attention turned towards the street. A snow plow hadn't passed through yet. He wondered how long they needed to wait, worrying about Brittany arriving at work safely.

Before long, Tessa wheeled around the corner with two plates. She placed one in front of him and sat across from him with her meal.

"On a normal day, I could only make an egg and cheese sandwich, but a customer special ordered maple bacon donuts for tomorrow."

"Well, I thank you for dipping into your supply." He looked down at the croissant, noting the fluffy folded egg, whitish-yellow cheese, and strips of bacon. "All this is missing is-"

"A slice of tomato," they said at the same time, laughing at the coincidence.

"Is this the same cheese you use on your danishes?" he asked.

She shook her head. "Oh, heaven's no. I use cream cheese for those. This is the same Asiago I use on my bagels."

He lifted the sandwich and took a large bite. The crunch from the croissant filled the otherwise silent room. "It's good," he said with a full mouth.

"That's great to hear," she said, digging into her own sandwich.

They sat and ate in companionable silence for a few minutes before Dalton asked, "It's slow today. Do you need Brittany? I would hate for her to risk driving in this weather if she doesn't need to."

Tess glanced through the window. "Probably not. I normally get more customers by now, but the passing cars aren't slowing down."

"It's the weather. It will pick up tomorrow for certain."

"You're right. Let me call Brittany. Then, I'd love to chat about my ideas for new breakfast and lunch dishes. These sandwiches inspired me."

"I would love to hear about it."

SPOOKED

THE SHOP'S BELL RANG AS DALTON entered. He smiled when he heard Tess shout from the back.

"Be right there!"

He used the wait to wipe his shoes on the mat and shake rain off his coat. Once finished, he stood waiting near the register. He glanced at his phone, reading the title of an email before swiping it away. He would unsubscribe one day, but he'd rather not deal with it now.

"Sorry about that," Tess said as she strode towards him. She grabbed a cup to get his usual coffee. "How's my favorite customer?"

He chuckled and shook his head. "No need to rush."

She popped the lid on the mug and placed it on the counter. "What would you like to eat?"

Over the last few months, he'd learned her routines, and she never acted this way. He mentally willed her to look at him while a coil of dread formed in his gut. "Tessa, what's wrong?"

"Nothing," she said, glancing up at him for a second before looking back down at the pastry case. "I'd recommend the red velvet cupcakes. They're my specialty."

Dalton sighed. He didn't want to push the subject, but something was amiss. Ignoring his coffee, he walked around the island between them and looped his arm with hers. For a few steps, her movements were hesitant, but she quickly recovered and followed his lead. Good. If she didn't, he would've carried her regardless of matters like dignity or whether or not she was his wife.

After they were in private, he pulled away to an arm's length and gave her a once over. She kept looking away from him, so he nudged her chin gently with his forefinger. He felt blinding rage only once before. He distinctly remembered the impossibility of controlling such wild emotion. The only reason he kept himself in check was Tessa's presence. Otherwise, nothing could stop his warpath as he sought to eviscerate the scum unworthy of disgracing the bottom of his boot.

"Who did this to you?" he asked in an inflectionless tone, barely keeping his anger from boiling over. He couldn't afford to scare her.

"Nobody. I'm accident prone. You know that," she said, swatting his hand away.

His eyebrows drew together. While he remembered her injuring her back and Brittany commenting about bruises, he never saw her stumble. She wasn't clumsy in the least. As pieces slotted themselves into place, he clenched his fists, imagining them pummeling into Cody's face one after the other.

"Stop, I know what you're thinking," she began, but he interrupted her.

"You don't get a bruised eye that needs to be covered up from nothing and no one. If you won't talk to me, that's fine. I'll call the authorities, and they will ensure the person who did this is behind bars where they belong," he said, grabbing his phone and searching for the non-emergency number for the local police.

She grabbed his arm, her eyes wide as she tried to wrestle the device from him. "No! Please don't. This is my fault. He didn't want to hurt me."

"A good husband doesn't hurt you, Tessa. He won't guilt or gaslight you. He loves and supports you unconditionally. You deserve better. You deserve-" he stopped himself from confessing his love. She deserved better than a murderer. Did she need a vampire who considered himself above the man she fell in love with? Her pure soul belonged with someone worthier than him, but if she would have him, he wouldn't hesitate.

The front bell rang. Dalton pocketed his phone and strode away. He packed a box with six muffins and sent the happy customer on their way without payment. When he returned, he rummaged through the freezer and retrieved a bag of ice. He made an ice pack and wrapped a towel around it before handing it to her.

He sighed as she placed it over the puffy area. "You're good with makeup. If you hadn't acted strangely, I might not have noticed. You need to report this to the authorities, and if you don't, I will. I care too much about you to let this continue. It will keep happening until he takes it too far. You need to understand that he will kill you."

"It's not like that!"

"Call an elephant an elephant. Abuse is abuse." He grabbed the shop phone and handed it to her. "Call Brittany and ask her to come in early. You need to file a police report."

Tess shook her head. "No. I can't. You don't understand."

"All I see is that my- friend," he ground out the word, "is getting hurt by the person who was never supposed to injure her in the first place, and she's defending the cretin." Dalton sighed and dialed the number on his phone. "I'm sorry, but if you won't report him, I will."

"Riverside police department. This is Cody. How can I direct your call?"

Dalton cleared his throat. "Sorry, I mis-dialed. Have a good day."

Without another word, he hung up. Now, he understood why she hadn't reported her husband.

Vision Turning Red

MAINTAINING A STOIC FAÇADE DESPITE his seething rage took a concerted effort. Tonight, he would destroy the fool, but right now, he needed to ensure Tessa's health and safety.

"Are you injured anywhere else?" he asked with false calm. If he allowed his emotions to run rampant, he'd scare her.

From her expression alone, he already had.

"Tess, I would never hurt you. My anger is not at you but the one who raised a hand to you.

I need to know the extent of the damage. You may require medical attention and not know it."

She wrung her hands together before she said, "It's just my face, Dalton."

He watched her expression as she spoke, and he decided she wasn't lying. He checked the time. "Do you have anywhere safe to go this evening?"

When she shook her head, he wasn't surprised. How many times had he heard about abusers isolating their victims so they felt they didn't have anywhere to go? His heart broke for her. He wanted to pull her into his arms and hold her until she'd cried herself out. She held this burden alone for too long. He sent a silent prayer for Cody to receive the punishment he deserved.

"How about Brittany? Would she let you stay with her?"

"I don't know. We get along, but I'm her boss. We just work together."

"If you explained what was happening, would she? And, if you don't want to talk to her about it, I can do it for you."

He knew he sounded overly formal, but he preferred it over his every word coming laced with anger. After everything she'd been through, he never wanted her to feel fear again. It would break him to cause her such agony.

Once again, she shook her head. "She has kids. It wouldn't be fair."

"Tessa, there are people who love you and want to help you. If I need to prove it to you, so be it."

He realized that, if his life were one of those romance books or movies women enjoyed, this should be the moment he professed his love and devotion. He would cradle her tenderly between his fingers and kiss her like he wanted to all along. His centuries old sense of propriety kept him in check. Their relationship was strictly platonic up to this point. Besides, she was married. Now was not the time, even if it ached not to make her his.

He realized he'd gotten far too close. The beating of her heart sang to him. Each pulsing beat lured him in like a siren's call, drawing him towards ruin. No, he was already destroyed. This woman dragged him under long ago, and she didn't even know. Despite being a supernatural predator, he was helpless to prevent it. As much as he considered Tessa his, he belonged to her in kind. She was both his salvation and his damnation. He just hoped to be worthy of her when she was his again.

Dalton took a step back. It pained him to pull away, but if he lingered, he would wrap her body in his own and never let go. Instead, he extended a hand. "May I please have your phone?"

The bell at the front of the shop rang, but Tess's eyes didn't break away. With a sigh, she unlocked the device.

When she handed it to him, she said, "I am trusting you with this. Don't make me regret it."

She plastered on a smile and strode out of the kitchen.

He stared at the phone, but he dare not linger for fear of having it time out and lock. After a couple clicks and swipes, he found Brittany's contact information. He hesitated again, trying to make a dozen decisions in short order. Should he use Tessa's phone or his? Would a call or a text be appropriate?

Somehow, he shook off the indecision and texted her with Tessa's phone.

Is it okay to call?

The seconds he waited for a response were infinite. When the phone pinged in his hand, it startled him. That was fast.

Yeah, I'll call you in a second. Dropping the spawn off at kiss and go.

He stared at the second sentence, trying to interpret it. Those were all English words, but in that order, they meant nothing to him.

Before he could think about it too deeply, the phone rang. He didn't prepare for the conversation. Unfortunately, being a shut-in didn't equip him to deal with people. He would have to play it by ear.

"No time like the present," he said as he swiped the icon to answer. "Hello, Brittany. This is Dalton."

"What's wrong? Who are we burying? Do I need to bring a shovel?" she asked in rapidfire.

He couldn't help but laugh. His instincts told him that Brittany was a good person; her reaction only confirmed his gut feeling.

"Nothing that dramatic, but Tessa needs a soft place to land tonight. Would you mind letting her stay at your place?"

"Of course! All she ever needed to do was ask," she said without pause.

"Thank you. I'm sure she'll explain when she's ready. I appreciate your help."

"I would do anything for Tess. She's a good person and a great boss."

He nodded before remembering they were on the phone. "I couldn't agree more. See you at the shop soon. Take care."

He hung up the phone and powered it off, handing it back to Tessa when he exited the kitchen. "Don't turn this back on today. If anybody asks why they can't reach you, tell them the battery died," he whispered.

She nodded and took the phone, but said nothing.

"You're going to be okay, but it may take time for you to feel that way."

"I hope you're right," she said under her breath. Her tears welled up, threatening to spill over.

Dalton placed a hand on her shoulder and gave the tiniest squeeze he could muster. "I promise to protect you. Always."

"And forever?" she asked in an instant, as if she didn't think the words.

He stiffened. Clearly, some part of Vanessa lived in her reincarnation. There was no way for her to understand the significance of her words otherwise.

"And forever," he said, stepping away and taking his forgotten coffee over to his table.

B⚭GEYMAN

DALTON STAYED AT THE BAKERY ALL DAY. He tried to remain unassuming, but he couldn't help but to scan the room every five minutes. Even though he doubted Cody would make an appearance, his muscles coiled tight, ready to pounce at the tiniest provocation. Men who used their strength and power to harm those weaker than them for no other reason than their own gratification were the vilest creatures on this planet, vampires like him included. He hated himself for letting this happen, but now that he knew the truth, he planned on arranging a meeting between Tessa's husband and the gods.

Throughout the day, he plotted exactly how he would go about the dark deed while bringing no suspicion onto the woman he loved. It would take a delicate touch, but if he did it right, she would be safe and none the wiser about the unfortunate but happy accident he orchestrated.

He did his best to check on Tessa without drawing too much attention to himself, but she caught him staring frequently. Her expression was unreadable but not because she wore an emotionless mask. It was quite the opposite. Based on her body language, her mood alternated between gratitude, fear, anxiety, and depression. It made him wonder what she was thinking, especially when her most significant glances seemed to coincide with his morbid thoughts about his role in Cody's untimely demise. Was he causing her anxiety, or did his presence remind her of her circumstances? He never wanted to cause her further distress. If he could, he would take away her pain instead.

By day's end, he escorted the ladies to Brittany's home safely before heading home himself. He gave Tessa instructions to wait until thirty minutes after Cody's shift to contact the police station and report him. With any luck, the police officer taking her statement would become her alibi while he dispatched the bastard.

Dalton's thirst for blood was never stronger. He wanted to show that vile excuse for a man a piece of his own medicine. He imagined pushing Cody against the wall and punching him bloody. Abusers deserved to experience what they doled out twice over, but what he wanted to do and what he should do were very different things. Unfortunately, succumbing to his basest desires would look premeditated, which it was. But the police didn't need to know that. The last thing he wanted to do was subject Tessa to a grueling police investigation.

She deserved better than she'd received from the man she'd fallen for. The least he could do was make her husband's death look accidental.

He parked in his carport but didn't linger there long. During her lunch break, he grilled

Tessa about Cody's habits. It turned out he often went to the bar after work, which served him well. A drunk man crashing a vehicle rarely made headlines nowadays. Of course, it happening to a cop in such a small town would likely rock the place to its core, but it shouldn't raise any red flags about foul play.

Dalton locked his car and walked towards the tavern in question. It was about a mile from his place, which wasn't far from the police station. Regardless of distance, he didn't want to drive to the watering hole. He'd seen too many idiots get behind the wheel of a motor vehicle while blitzed out of their mind, and he loved his car too much to risk it.

Besides, he already knew about one car accident happening tonight; he planned to orchestrate it. Cody made his choices, and his life was forfeit.

He arrived at the bar just as the first drops of rain fell from the sky. The irony almost made him laugh. Didn't all the best murder mysteries start with the line, *it was a dark and stormy night*?

He wiped his shoes before wandering over to a bar stool. Several people glanced his way before returning to their drinks and conversation.

The bartender finished up with another customer before sauntering over. "Hey there, bud. Do you know what you'll be drinking tonight?"

"Jack and Coke," Dalton said without hesitation. The whiskey wasn't his favorite brand, but it was widely available in America. He never had an issue ordering it.

"Got it. Want a menu or are you just drinkin' tonight?"

He shook his head. "Just the drinks for now, but I'll let you know if I change my mind."

The bartender gave him a quick two-fingered salute before working on Dalton's drink. It didn't take long. He slid a coaster over and placed the drink on top.

"Just this one for ya, or do you want to open a tab?"

"Better open a tab."

He nodded and opened his hand. "I'll be needing your ID, then."

Dalton reached into his back pocket and fished his driver's license out of his wallet.

"Thank you," he said, picking up his beverage and taking a sip.

The bartender watched and waited expectantly. "That a good pour for you or do you like it more or less heavy-handed?"

"This is good."

The bartender nodded and punched things in on the nearby till.

Dalton gazed into his drink, afraid to look at someone the wrong way and bring himself unwanted attention. He needed to blend into the background. People would know he'd been here, but he wanted to be a footnote rather than a chapter.

Now, the hardest part of the night was upon him.

Waiting.

When he considered his life after death objectively, his existence was a study in waiting, but for this, he grew impatient. Every second Cody lived could cause Tessa more harm. She was too important to let him linger in this life a moment longer than necessary.

The front door opened, and Dalton couldn't help but look. It was a false alarm. He expected his quarry to arrive soon, though. With each passing moment, his desire to eradicate the law enforcement officer who thought he could get away with one of the most heinous crimes grew. His bloodlust never worked itself into such a fever pitch. If he didn't taste vengeance soon, even horror movies would struggle to duplicate the trail of carnage he created.

Once again, a rush of cool air blew past as another guest entered the tavern. It took a Herculean effort to keep his attention on his drink. He wanted to look unassuming and disinterested, but he severely underestimated the task's difficulty.

"Evening, Rick. Can I get the usual?"

He knew that voice. To check without drawing attention to himself, he picked up his glass and sipped, sneaking a peek as he did so. He wanted to pump his fist in triumph, but he somehow restrained himself.

A few words passed between the bartender and Cody, but he didn't hear them. He was too wrapped up in his murderous thoughts.

"Oh, hey. How're you doing, man?" Cody asked.

Dalton looked up and smiled, hoping it looked convincing. It still grated his nerves that

Cody never learned his name or even bothered to worry about it like Tessa and Brittany had, but he couldn't linger on such things right now. To keep things casual, he shrugged.

"Rough day," he said honestly. "Got some bad news. Just needed to unwind, you know?"

Cody clapped him on the shoulder, sitting down beside him. "I get that. You came to the right place. Rick will help you feel better in no time."

He laughed. "I don't doubt that. My drink is strong."

"Good to hear. What're you up to? Anything new?"

"Not really. My job is on autopilot and has been for years. A close friend shared some terrible news, and it's something I wish I could help with. Hit me harder than I thought it would, I suppose."

Rick, the bartender, placed a pint of beer in front of Cody and asked, "We startin' ya a tab today?"

Dalton shook his head. "His drinks are on me this time. I owe him. He's helped me more than once."

The man nodded and walked over to the register to ring up the drink.

"Did you want to talk about your friend or is this a getting your mind off of things type of night?"

"I need to drag myself out of the darkness," he said, feeling a thrill as Cody fell into his trap.

"That's what I thought. Distractions are the best way to get your head on straight. Want to play darts?"

"Why not?"

They grabbed the darts from a shelf beside the board. It took them a few turns to find a rhythm of throwing the dart and updating their scores.

Dalton eyed Cody's drink, noting how quickly he made it disappear. Maybe alcoholism caused the man's indiscretions, but he refused to give him the benefit of the doubt and allow him the chance to reform. As soon as he laid a finger on Tessa, he wrote himself a one-way ticket to hell.

He extricated himself from the game long enough to order each of them a second drink. When the coroner ran toxicology on Cody later, he wanted to make sure his blood alcohol showed him as good and knackered. He returned to their game with both drinks in hand.

"Thanks for getting my mind off of things tonight," he lied. "This'll probably be my last one. I walked here, and it's getting pretty bad out there."

"Oh, do you need a ride home? I don't mind it, if you're wanting to chill longer."

He held up his hand to stop the other man. "No, I couldn't impose. Walking clears my head. I don't mind."

"Alright. Let me know if you change your mind."

"It's not a problem."

They played another round, and Cody won a second time.

"Wow. You must play a lot."

"I play enough. Not as good as some of the competitive players, but I hold my own against casual opponents."

"Good to know. Next, you'll tell me you're a card shark too."

Cody laughed. "Only against my coworkers. I lose money at the casino."

"Well, you'd best me without a doubt. Do you want me to buy you another?" he asked, pointing at Cody's half-empty brew. The man could really put them away.

"I don't think I know how to turn free drinks down."

Dalton laughed, "Be right back."

He walked to the counter and set his glass down. He didn't care to finish it anymore.

"Hey, Rick. Could you get one more for Cody, and after that, I'd like to settle my tab." He reached into his wallet and handed him a debit card.

The bartender grabbed the card, rang up the beer, and completed the transaction. He handed Dalton the receipt before pouring Cody another cold one. As Dalton calculated a tip, he slid over the beverage.

"Don't be a stranger," Rick said with a kind smile.

He nodded and took the drink.

"I'm going to head out," he said, handing Cody the beer.

"Alright. You know where to find me if you need anything. Have a good night."

"You as well."

Dalton waved and headed out the door with little fanfare. Now, his actual plan began. It seemed counterintuitive, but he walked home. His steps were faster than before, but between the worsening weather and his goal, he made them all with purpose.

The police would open an investigation later tonight, and he didn't want them to suspect foul play even for a moment. He must protect Tessa at all costs, which meant this entire scheme needed to look accidental.

He arrived home and intentionally used his front door, making sure the doorbell camera filmed him entering. Once he got inside, he locked the door, ditched his phone, and walked all the way through to the back. When he stepped outside, he transformed into his bat form and flew back to the bar.

Earlier on, he asked Tessa for a description of Cody's vehicle, and he was grateful for his foresight. If he tried spotting Cody's car from inside, it would likely set off alarm bells in the night's aftermath. Having the information he needed made his last steps child's play.

He shifted his body into mist and used his newfound mobility to squeeze his way through the vehicle's less than airtight crevices. In seconds, he was inside. The process disoriented him, and he often avoided using the ability. Once he regained his bearings, he transformed back into a bat again and took cover in shadow.

Now, all he needed to do was wait.

Outside, the sun set, and the winter chill overtook the world. The overcast day allowed the night's darkness to swallow the town in its maw. There were little more than street lights to illuminate the parking lot.

It surprised Dalton how long Cody spent drinking before he left. He couldn't get a good look without risk of revealing his location, but he guessed another hour passed while the man scuttled away his pay with drink. At least, the cop would be very inebriated.

The car door finally opened and with it came the stench of liquor and sweat. His quarry was three sheets to the wind.

This would be easy.

Cody started the car. He placed his hands over the warming air vents before rubbing them together and patting his cheeks.

"Alright. Pull it together. You've got this."

He put the car in reverse. With practiced ease for somebody so drunk, he maneuvered his way out of the parking lot and onto the main road.

Dalton took on his human form. He crouched out of sight, but he could see the street now. When they reached a curve in the road ahead of them, he planned to make his move. He leaned in as they approached, prepared to strike.

Cody must've spotted him in his peripheral vision or mirror. Before Dalton could end the man's miserable life, the car swerved and its driver screamed.

"No time like the present," Dalton muttered, bashing the man's head into the steering wheel using an open hand.

The scent of fresh blood filled his nostrils, but he didn't have the time to savor the scent. He had a job to do, not a meal to eat. Reaching over the center console, he pressed Cody's right leg down. The car rocketed forward.

He spotted the man's seatbelt. Unbuckled. He'd never put it on. A fatal mistake.

The car hopped the curb, jerking as they careened into a grassy drainage ditch. Dalton gripped the steering wheel and helped guide the vehicle directly into a tree. They hit two seconds later. The car jerked to a stop, windshield shattering.

Cody's limp, unconscious body flew out. Dalton heard a crack when his body struck the tree. The man's heart stuttered. He would be dead before anybody contacted the authorities.

Dalton pulled out a handkerchief and wiped the steering wheel clean of fingerprints. He pocketed the piece of fabric and transformed into a bat one last time, flying home.

Only destruction remained in his wake.

Vᴀᴍᴘɪʀɪᴄ Lᴏᴠᴇ

WHEN DALTON ARRIVED AT THE BAKERY AT his usual time the next morning, he was surprised to find the lights off. His eyebrows drew together. The storefront never looked so abandoned when he arrived. He stepped back and pulled his phone out to check the time.

Perhaps, he was earlier than usual. He checked the time on his phone against the hours on the sign. There was no reason for the door to be locked. They didn't move daylight savings to January, did they?

Behind him, somebody cleared their throat.

He turned around to find Tessa there. She wore jeans and a puffy jacket. She skipped her makeup, so he could see the bruising Cody caused. His heart stuttered out a jagged beat before he calmed himself. That cretin could never hurt her again.

He noticed the puffiness around her eyes and the tear stains on her cheeks. His heart sank. He caused this, and what he'd done wasn't the type of thing he could take back. A wave of nerves shook him when he realized he was the one who took away her autonomy. He'd grown too possessive, and he protected her by taking away her ability to choose.

He was no better than Cody.

"We're closed today," she said, interrupting his thoughts, "and possibly forever."

He didn't know how to respond. All he could do was stare and think to himself that, despite everything, she was beautiful.

"I'm sorry, but I'm afraid I don't understand," he finally said after a long moment of hesitation. His speech sounded stiff, even to him, but he needed to know what was going on. What was he missing here?

"Cody passed away last night," she said as she stepped around him and taped a sign that read, Closed until further notice, on the door.

"I'm sorry to hear that," he said without missing a beat. "If there's anything I can do-"

"You've done enough, Dalton," she muttered, jabbing him in the chest with a finger. The action was an accusation. "This is not what I wanted. I did not ask for this. I would've been fine after reporting him to the authorities."

He raised his hands facing forward on either side of his head in surrender. "I don't know what it is you're talking-"

"I know it was you! I just do. Everything was fine before you. I was fine."

"Tessa, I-"

"Stop it! Just stop. I don't know what this is, but I will not play a part in your sick little game any longer."

"I don't know what you think I did, but I am so sorry for your loss. Please, if there's anything I can do for you-"

She shook her head, glaring up at him with white-hot anger burning in her eyes. "Just go,

Dalton. Leave and never come back, and if you don't leave, I will."

"I- Tessa, I don't understand."

She huffed a frustrated growl and poked him in the chest like she might spear somebody with a lance, as if the tip of her finger were her weapon of choice. "I don't know why, but I can sometimes hear your thoughts. And before you say something about figuring it out together, I don't want to know why. I just want you gone. I want my peaceful life from before you ever came here back."

"What?" the word fell out of him. He didn't even think about saying it. It happened all on its own.

"I heard you think about planning to kill Cody, and I want nothing to do whatever this is," she said, pointing between the two of them. Her entire body deflated a moment later, like all the fight and rage bubbling up inside completely flooded out of her after somebody released a dam of pent-up emotions.

"Just go," she whispered, eyes spilling over with fresh tears. "I didn't want this. I don't want you."

Her words struck him like a punch to the gut. One last time, his traitorous heart beat. For her. He knew it would always only beat for her.

Before he left, he needed to say it at least once. He had to tell her.

"I love you," he said. "I always have."

"Your love isn't what I want or need right now. You can have your love, but I can't trust you, Dalton. Please, just go."

He nodded and walked away from the love of his existence. It was the single hardest thing he'd ever done in his long life, including laying her first incarnation to rest. He drove away as an aching pain bloomed in his chest. One of his hands rubbed the spot absently as he tried to figure out where he went wrong. There was so much to unpack about the entire encounter. How could she hear his thoughts? When did it start? What did she hear?

His thoughts kept circling back around to one thing: Hope. Cursed, wretched hope. He was tired of hoping, but it was all he could muster. If she was truly his as deeply as he believed she was, she would want him back, and he would always wait, ready to be her lover or her protector or her friend, no matter what.

Acknowledgements

The last couple of years, and this book especially, have taken me on a weird journey. From hopping between one pen name then another to moving to an entirely different state, I have so many reasons and people to be thankful for.

To Jeff and Sara, who had to listen to me whining about wanting to write a book that was "worth a damn." I'm sure you were both getting sick of me complaining about my inability to write something that meant something to somebody rather than some "asinine romantic drivel." I appreciate you both tolerating me, even when this book still turned out to be a romance at its heart. LOL.

My wholehearted thanks to Chelsi, my sister in everything but blood, who started writing books with tragic (or at least less-than-happy) endings right around the same time as me. It takes a certain amount of courage to subvert readers' genre expectations rather than writing something "marketable" for the sake of it. You led the way and helped show me it was possible to write what you loved, wanted, and needed to write without conforming to the expectations of others.

For Linn, a.k.a. Dragon Lady, who is always there to share knowledge, triumphs, commiseration, and spreadsheets... so many spreadsheets. I appreciate your willingness to always talk shop and statistics, analytics, etc. I'm so very glad I know you outside of a professional setting. I always enjoy our late night or early morning tea and coffee fueled chats. It's a shame that all of my friends have to live in Narnia or something.

To Deni, who I keep harassing about whether my book covers are good enough. I'm sorry I'm like this. It won't change, but I *am* sorry. Your knowledge and feedback are invaluable. Our bond over our similar AuDHD idiosyncrasies brings me so much joy. Give the animals love from me. Oh, and Scott, I'm sorry for all the times she shows you the memes I send and they make you spray coffee out of your nose.

Thank you to the squad (listed in no particular order): Courtney, Jade, Mel, Matt, Ellie, Kolbi, and Cassie. Sorry if I missed somebody. You guys have been with me through a lot, and you make it difficult for the author to express the right words of appreciation and love.

For my adoptive mothers Karen and Brenda, I know in my heart that I could've carried on without you, but I'm so very glad that I didn't have to. You have made me feel so very loved and accepted when I have most needed it. Being able to lean on you when I am weak has been a blessing.

For the survivors. Never forget what made you find your voice, and never let them take it again. The national domestic violence hotline number is 1-800-799-7233.

And finally, to my readers: An author can't exist without readers, and for you, I am eternally grateful. I would've given up long ago if it weren't for your support. Every time I see another purchase or review, I get a little thrill of excitement that somebody found my words and I hope they enjoy them. I don't think that feeling will ever go away. If you enjoyed this novelette, please consider leaving a review on your favorite book review website or with the retailer you purchased from.

DELETED SCENE

MOST MORNINGS, DALTON LEFT AFTER Brittany arrived for her shift, but the way she walked in the door on this particular day caused him to hesitate.

The bell over the door rang, and the door clacked with the force Tessa's assistant put into opening it. She pointed at her boss with fire in her eyes.

"You are in so much trouble. Did you think you could get away with not telling me it's your birthday next week?"

Tessa's eyes were wide, like a startled doe in the woods. In her surprise, her hand gripped the center of her chest.

The entire bakery fell silent while they waited to see the drama unfold. For a few charged moments, Dalton thought he may need to intervene, but after several long seconds, the proprietor recovered.

"I didn't want to make a fuss over it."

Brittany finally noticed their audience and took an intentional breath.

"Okay, so we're doing a big bash for your birthday, right? Buy a half dozen cupcakes, get a seventh free? Or maybe we could do birthday cake-pop bouquets? Or-"

"Please stop. I don't want a big celebration, and I don't like cake. It's not a big deal to me. Christmas is in two weeks. I usually celebrate my birthday in July."

"Heck no, girl!" Brittany started getting excitable again.

Tessa balled her hands into fists, but it was the only outward sign of frustration she showed.

"I don't like cake, so I'm not interested in doing anything more cake related than we already do."

"What?! You can't not have cake for your birthday."

"If it's my birthday, I'm not eating cake."

Dalton covered up a chuckle behind his hand with a cough. This was the typical, obstinate as a boar Vanessa he knew centuries ago. He was glad he waited to leave. In fact, he would've paid pay-per-view prices to watch this show.

Brittany had obviously entered the bargaining stages of grief because in her next breath, she asked, "Then, what treat can I make for you?"

Tessa audibly sighed and made a flippant hand gesture. "Cheesecake."

"Cheesecake is cake, honey."

"Oh no, it's not. Cheesecake is a pie, and I will fight and die on this hill."

"It has the word cake in the name. Cheese cake, get it?"

Dalton immediately knew Brittany was in trouble when Tessa waggled her forefinger at her. At this point, he gave up bothering to cover his grin. He could tell it reached his eyes already.

"Oh no, it's not," Tessa said, mimicking Brittany's words. "Cheesecake is a pie. It has a crust. No cake has a crust."

"I can't even believe we're arguing over the semantics of whether cheesecake is a cake while we're completely ignoring the fact that you also said you don't want to make a big deal out of your birthday."

"You're the one who started the conversation in the first place, but if you must know, celebrating a birthday around the holidays is the worst. That's why I wait to celebrate. It doesn't hurt my feelings. Chill out."

Brittany huffed and made her way into the back. When she returned, she said, "Fine. Then, I will make you a cheesepie."

Tessa made a face. "Don't call it that."

"You're the one who started the cheesecake is pie argument," she mocked in response.

Dalton stood and cleared his table. As he headed towards the door, Dalton said, "Cheesecake is actually a tart."

He didn't wait around to find out the chaos he caused, but from the scandalized screams, he knew both Brittany and Tessa would be feverishly debating the merits of this newfound information all day.

About the Author

Maria Caiazza is a semi-professional, semi-crazed author who lives off of caffeine and spite. Her pen names are Maria Caiazza and M. W. McLeod. She loves exploring the line between what makes a hero or a villain and writing about morally grey characters she can't necessarily agree with. She writes modern fairy tale retellings and other tales with a dark twist.

Want all the news about more works by Maria Caiazza?
Join her mailing list here:
https://subscribepage.io/uPXPSm

Find Maria on her socials here:
https://beacons.ai/mariacaiazzaauthor